Cuffy's New York City Adventure

Eifrig Publishing LLC

Lemont   Berlin

Published by Eifrig Publishing,
PO Box 66, 701 Berry Street, Lemont, PA 16851, USA
Knobelsdorffstr. 44, 14059 Berlin, Germany.

For information regarding permission, write to:
Rights and Permissions Department,
Eifrig Publishing,
PO Box 66, Lemont, PA 16851, USA.
permissions@eifrigpublishing.com, +1-888-340-6543

 Library of Congress Control Number: 2012949875

Lisa Marie Foto.
Cuffy's New York City Adventure/
by Lisa Marie Foto, Nancy J. Goldberg & Susan Mandell
 illustrated by Andrea Strongwater
p. cm.

Paperback: ISBN 978-1-936172-65-8
Hard cover: ISBN 978-1-936172-66-5

[I. New York City – Juvenille Fiction. 2. Self-image – Juvenille Fiction.
3. Animals – Tigers.]

I. Strongwater, Andrea, ill. II. Title

2017 16 15 14 13
5 4 3 2 1

Printed on acid-free paper. ∞

To our families for encouragement,
our students for their inspiration,
and to our friendship,
which continues to be adventurous!
LMF, NJG, SM

Cuffy, school was so awesome today!
At circle time, my friend Marc told us about
his trip to New York City.

He said his favorite place was the
ginormous statue of a lady who stands in the harbor.
Marc had to take a ferry to get up close.

Wow, I really want to see her, too!

Mom always says,
"Spencer, tip your red cap,
so you can see where you are going."

I don't know why . . .

I know where I'm
going now!

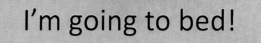

I'm going to bed!

Could this really be?
I must be dreaming!

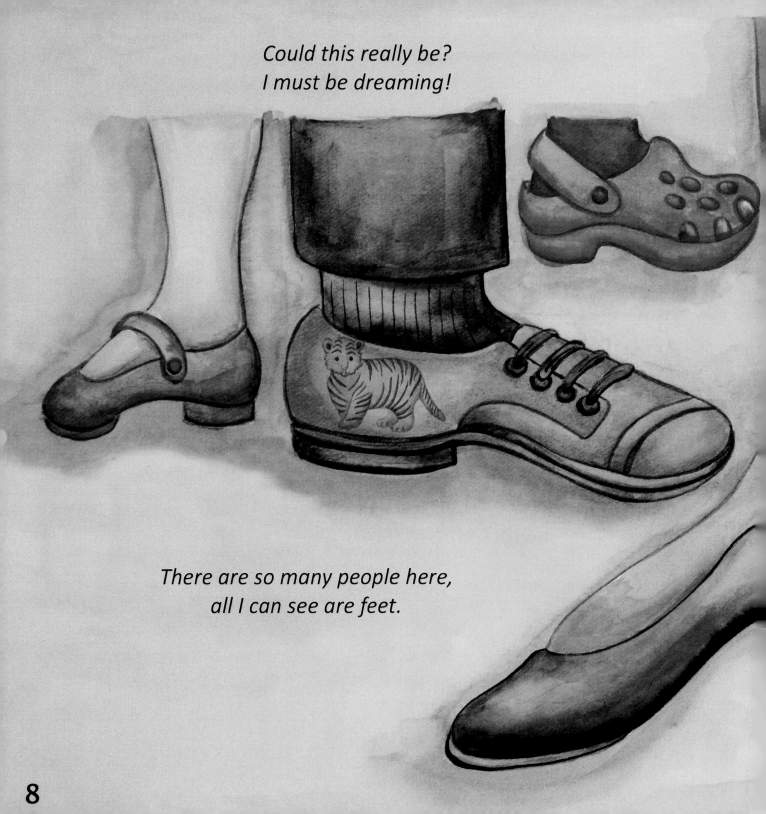

There are so many people here,
all I can see are feet.

8

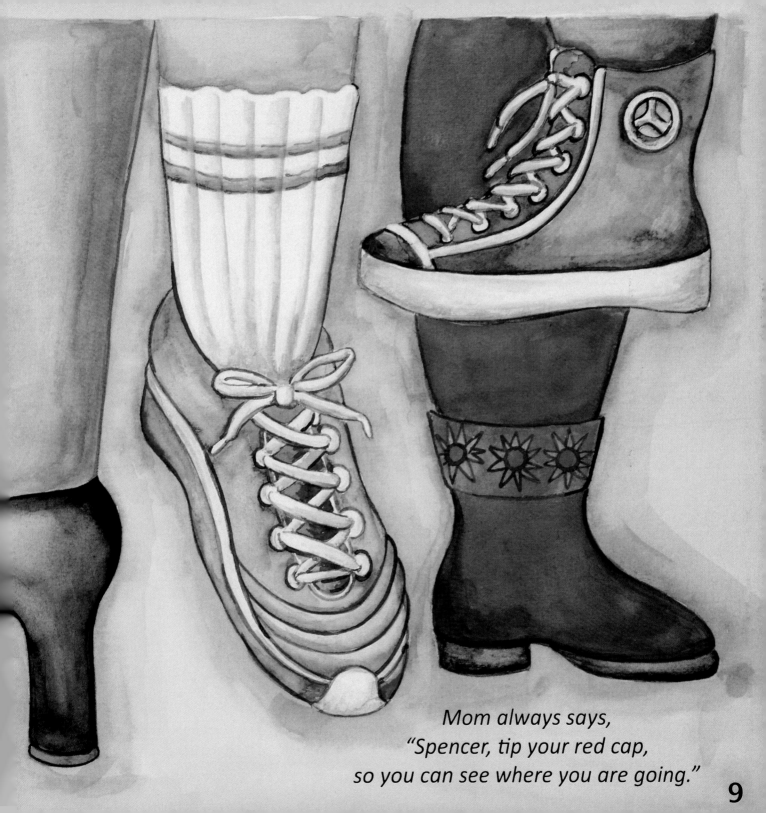

Mom always says,
"Spencer, tip your red cap,
so you can see where you are going."

9

Wow, I'm in
Grand Central Station
in New York City!

I can't believe it, this is great!
Look at all those stars!

11

Just look at all the people!
I wonder which way I should go?
I want to find that tall lady, the Statue of Liberty.

Do I go uptown?
Do I go downtown?
I wonder what
Cuffy would do?

Mom always says,
"Spencer, tip your red cap,
so you can see where
you are going."

I'm going up the stairs and out to the street.
New York City, here I come!

They are gigantic! I will ask my Uncle Larry, who is an architect, how they build such tall buildings.

Where am I now? Skating in the middle of New York City?
How can that be?

16

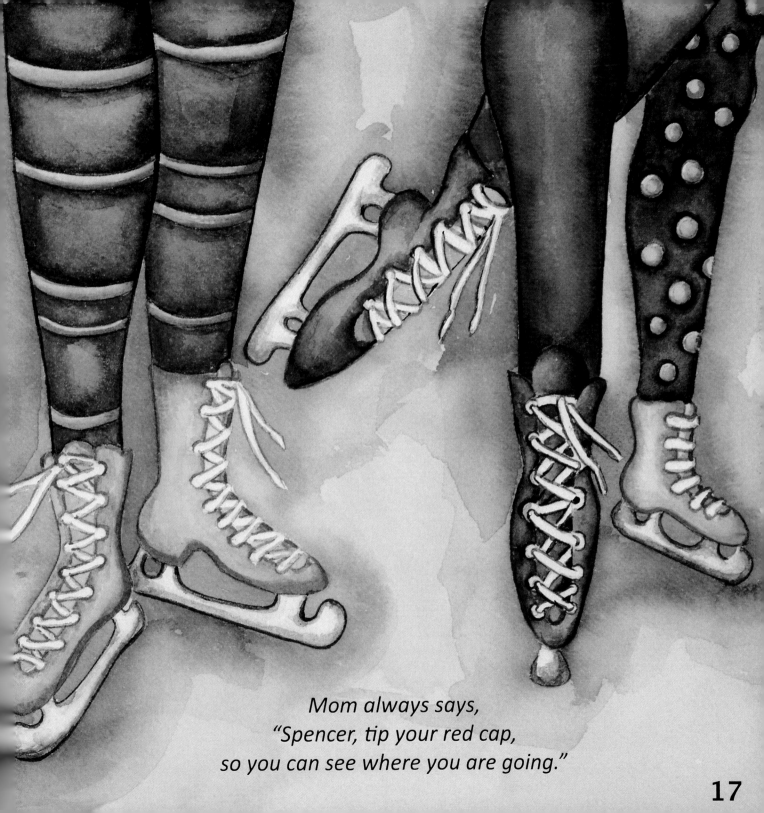

Mom always says,
"Spencer, tip your red cap,
so you can see where you are going."

All these different flags and ice skating.
I must be at Rockefeller Center.

This looks like fun,
but I really want to see the Statue of Liberty.

18

So, I think I'll keep going.
Maybe I should go downtown.

19

RANSIT

Wow, that must be a limousine.
I wonder what it would be
like to ride in one?

I really need to be careful crossing the busy street.
Mom always says, "Spencer, tip your red cap,
so you can see where you are going."

21

When the light is red, I know I have to stop and wait. Now
it is green. I'm on my way to find the Statue of Liberty.

Awesome!
Paws! Paws! They're just like Cuffy's! Here in New York City!
I can't believe it! Who do they belong to?

Mom always says, "Spencer, tip your red cap,
so you can see where you are going."

So many steps, giant paws, and big lions, too! Those paws belong to these lions! This must be the New York Public Library!

I would love to stay and read some books,
but I'm very busy today.
I guess I'll just keep on going.

Look at all the different stores!
There is so much to see and do in this great big city!
Will I ever find the Statue of Liberty?

STORE HOURS
MONDAY to SATURDAY
10 AM to 9 PM

OPEN TIL 9 PM
GIFTS ON NINE

I wonder what's behind these huge doors?
Mom always says, "Spencer, tip your red cap,
so you can see where you are going."

29

These BIG doors belong
to a VERY, VERY tall building
with a point at the top!
It looks like it could touch the clouds.

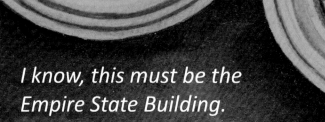

I know, this must be the
Empire State Building.

If I could go to the top, I could touch the clouds, be taller than a giant, and see the whole city, but I REALLY want to see the Statue of Liberty!

But what is this?
Water? A big ship?
What could this be?

Mom always says, "Spencer, tip your red cap, so you can see where you are going."

Such a big ship and jetplanes, too?

34

Now I know
that I must be at the
Intrepid Sea, Air & Space Museum.

Ahhh . . . Now I remember,
the Statue of Liberty is in New York Harbor.
I have to take a ferry to get there.
I need to keep going until I reach the pier.

There it is, I'm getting on board. This ride is lots of fun!

I'm getting closer.
Look at all those bricks.

This must be it!

Mom always says,
"Spencer, tip your red cap,
so you can see where
you are going."

I'm here! I'm here!
I see great big toes.
Wait, there's more!
I see her face,
her crown,
and the TORCH!

Wow, Marc was right. She is ginormous!
I want to go to the top.

C'mon Cuffy!
Let's go!

39

Dad, Dad, let me tell you about my AWESOME dream!
What an adventure!

I can't wait for school!

I'm going to share Cuffy and
my favorite red cap
at circle time.

All my friends will want to hold Cuffy,
because he is so soft and cuddly! When I hold him,
I feel adventurous, brave, and curious, just like him!